Katharine the Almost Great

The Purr-fect-o Present

by Lisa Mullarkey

illustrated by Phyllis Harris

magic Wagon

visit us at www.abdopublishing.com

In memory of three cool cats: Pumpkin, Spoinky, and Stanley. —LM
To Patty and Pam, my sisters who love their kitties —PH

Published by Magic Wagon, a division of the ABDO Group, PO Box 398166, Minneapolis, Minnesota 55439. Copyright © 2012 by Abdo Consulting Group, Inc. International copyrights reserved in all countries. All rights reserved. No part of this book may be reproduced in any form without written permission from the publisher.

Calico Chapter Books™ is a trademark and logo of Magic Wagon.

Printed in the United States of America, North Mankato, Minnesota.
092011
012012
 This book contains at least 10% recycled materials.

Text by Lisa Mullarkey
Illustrations by Phyllis Harris
Edited by Stephanie Hedlund and Rochelle Baltzer
Interior layout and design by Jaime Martens
Cover design by Jaime Martens

Library of Congress Cataloging-in-Publication Data
Mullarkey, Lisa.
    The purr-fect-o present / by Lisa Mullarkey ; illustrated by Phyllis Harris.
        p. cm. -- (Katharine the Almost Great)
    Summary: It is almost Christmas, but Katharine's teacher Mrs. Bingsley is unhappy--can Katharine discover why and find a present that will cheer her teacher up?
    ISBN 978-1-61641-831-1
    1. Gifts--Juvenile fiction. 2. Teachers--Juvenile fiction. 3. Schools--Juvenile fiction. 4. Christmas stories. [1. Gifts--Fiction. 2. Teachers--Fiction. 3. Schools--Fiction. 4. Christmas--Fiction.] I. Harris, Phyllis, 1962- ill. II. Title. III. Series: Mullarkey, Lisa. Katharine the almost great.
    PZ7.M91148Pu 2012
    813.6--dc23
                                                    2011026390

❋ CONTENTS ❋

CHAPTER 1

Miss Crankypants

"Not another one, Crockett!" I pressed my hand to my forehead and used my best Penelope Parks voice. "I simply can't take it anymore. No more jokes, dah-ling!"

But nothing would stop Crockett. He leaned forward and whispered, "What do elves learn in school?"

He didn't wait for an answer. "The elfabet." His eyes lit up. "Get it?"

Christmas was eight days away. That meant eight more days of Crockett's jokes!

I glanced at the Christmas tree in the reading corner. My heart thumpity thumped. I love Christmas! It's my very most favorite holiday. Along with Valentine's Day. And New Year's Eve. And my birthday, of course!

I wrinkled my eyes. "How many more Christmas jokes do you know?"

Crockett tap, tap, tapped his head. "Plenty." His hand shot into the air. "Mrs. Bingsley, can I tell some jokes before lunch?"

Mrs. Bingsley glanced at her watch. "Sure. I'd love to hear some."

Crockett jumped up. "What do snowmen eat for breakfast?"

"Frosted Flakes!" shouted Johnny.

Crockett gave Johnny two thumbs-up. "Here's one you won't know. How does Santa get to the dentist?"

No one knew the answer.

"On the Molar Express!" Crockett slapped his thigh. "Get it?"

Mrs. Bingsley groaned and smiled. "Got it!"

"How does a sheep say 'Merry Christmas' in Mexico?" asked Crockett.

"I know this one!" said Mrs. Bingsley. "Fleece Navidad."

I scooted closer to Mrs. Bingsley. "I have a joke. What do cats on the beach and Christmas have in common?"

Everyone tried to figure out the answer. Everyone except Mrs. Bingsley.

Her smile slid right off her face. Her shoulders drooped. "That's enough, kids. Lunchtime."

"Don't you want to know the answer?" I asked.

Everyone nodded.

Everyone except Mrs. Bingsley. Her mouth twitched and she shook her head. She lined us up and marched us down to the cafeteria.

"Is Mrs. Bingsley mad at you?" asked Vanessa when we sat at our table.

I chomped and chewed the crust off my sandwich. "I didn't do anything."

"Maybe she's mad that you didn't do your homework again," said Vanessa. "Or maybe she's mad that you spilled glitter on her desk. Or maybe . . ."

But Miss Priss-A-Poo didn't finish her sentence.

Crockett did. "Maybe she saw you write *Ho, Ho, Ho!* on your desk," he said.

I peeled the top off my yogurt. "At least the glitter was red. It's her favorite color, you know. Besides, she didn't see my desk. My letters were teensy-weensy."

Tamara slurped her milk. "Has anyone noticed that Mrs. Bingsley has been . . ." her eyes darted around the room, ". . . cranky?"

"Cranky with a capital C," I said. "Maybe we should call her Miss Crankypants."

"Call who Miss Crankypants?" asked a voice behind me.

My skin tingled when I saw my mom holding a tray of gingerbread cookies. My cheeks felt like they were as red as Rudolph's nose.

Crockett snatched a cookie off the tray. "I have a joke for you, Aunt Carol."

Mom laughed. "I thought you would."

"What did the Gingerbread Man put on his bed?"

Mom put her finger on her chin. "Hmmm, I don't know."

Crockett flashed a super-duper smile. "A cookie sheet!"

Mom laughed and handed Crockett a second cookie. "A good joke deserves another good cookie."

Then she narrowed her eyes. "Katharine, did I hear you call someone Miss Crankypants?"

Rebecca giggled. It was not a giggle moment.

I had to come up with one of my fab-u-lo-so facts from my 365 useless facts calendar. I twirl-a-whirled my hair around my finger.

"Did you know that gingerbread houses became popular in Germany during the nineteenth century after *Hansel and Gretel* was written?" I asked.

"Actually, I did know that," said Mom. Her watch beeped. "My veggie burgers!" She rushed toward the kitchen.

"I have an idea," said Vanessa. "Let's ask Mrs. Bingsley if we can have a Secret Santa!"

I jumped up and down. "That's a great idea! Mrs. Bingsley will love it!"

But Mrs. Bingsley didn't love the idea. Not one itty-bitty bit.

"What if we agreed to only spend $5.00?" I asked after recess. "Someone could buy me Purplicious Penelope Parks Nail Polish for $4.99." I puckered my lips. "Or some Pinklicious Lip Gloss for only $3.99."

At first, Mrs. Bingsley's eyes brightened. "I suppose $5.00 isn't too much money."

Everyone cheered and squealed. Crockett and Matthew did a chest bump. The celebration didn't last very long.

"Last year," said Vanessa, "my Secret Santa got me a Princess Kitty Diary. Princess Kitty is one cool cat!"

Mrs. Bingsley bit her lip. "Princess Kitty?" Her eyes watered. "Sorry, kids. I changed my mind. There won't be a Secret Santa this year."

Vanessa folded her arms and rocked back and forth.

"How about we bake gifts for each other instead?" said Rebecca.

"That won't work," said Mrs. Bingsley. "There are too many food allergies in our class."

Johnny sighed. "Yep! I'm allergic to peanuts."

"No chocolate for me," said Tamara. "And Rebecca can't have wheat."

Rebecca nodded and rubbed her stomach.

"And if I come within ten feet of an egg or even look at a chicken," said Matthew, "I blow up like a balloon."

"Let's focus on our stories now." Mrs. Bingsley scanned the room. "Matthew, would you please read yours first?"

Matthew cleared his throat. "*The Christmas Cat* by Matthew—"

Mrs. Bingsley reached for a tissue. "*The Christmas Cat*?"

Matthew nodded. Mrs. Bingsley looked at the clock. "Maybe we should have free reading time instead."

Crockett shrugged and walked over to the carpet. Vanessa scooted her chair closer to me and whispered, "What *do* cats on the beach and Christmas have in common?"

I giggled. "Sandy claws."

"Katharine!" said Mrs. Bingsley. "Shouldn't you be reading?"

I slid down in my seat and poked my nose into a book. A minute later, Vanessa tossed a note on my desk.

She really is Miss Crankypants.

I looked over at Mrs. Bingsley. She was mumbling to herself.

I traced over the *Ho! Ho! Ho!* on my desk and added two more words.

Bah.

Humbug!

❀ CHAPTER 2 ❀

News for Crockett

"Fess up, Katharine," said Mom. "Who were you calling Miss Crankypants?"

Dad looked confused. "Miss Cranky *what?*"

"Crankypants," said Crockett. He laughed.

Then Jack laughed. "Me, me, me." He threw his sippy cup on the ground. "More, more, more."

Aunt Chrissy swiped the cup off the floor. "Who's acting cranky? I hope it's not me."

"Me," said Jack as he reached for his sippy cup. "Me."

I tickled his toes. "No, Jack. You're a cutie pie. It's Mrs. Bingsley."

Mom's mouth fell open. "Mrs. Bingsley? I find that hard to believe. She's always so happy. Are you sure she's cranky?"

"I'm positively positive," I said. "She's been grump, grump, grumpy a lot lately." I reached for another pork chop. "She didn't like my joke today and I'm a funny girl."

"She didn't like Matthew's story either," said Crockett, shaking his head. "And he's a good writer."

Aunt Chrissy spoke up. "She can't like every story or think every joke is funny. Does that make her cranky?"

"She was going to let us have a Secret Santa this year but then she changed her mind," said Crockett. "Her class had one *last* year. Why not this year?"

"Because she's Miss Crankypants," I said. "As soon as Vanessa told the class what she got from her Secret Santa in second grade, she changed her mind."

Dad wiped his mouth. "What did Vanessa get? Maybe it wasn't appropriate."

"She got something *totally* appropriate," I said. "It was a Princess Kitty diary."

Dad smirked. A Princess-Kitty-Diary-is-a-silly-gift kind of smirk.

I poked his arm. "A diary is very educational, you know. It's like Writing Workshop."

"Fair enough," said Dad. "Maybe Mrs. Bingsley's the type that just doesn't like the holidays."

"She loves Christmas," said Crockett. "We have a tree in our reading corner and decorations are all over the walls. She even plays Christmas music."

Mom chimed in. "She did tell me she won her neighborhood door-decorating contest three years in a row. And if I'm not mistaken, she listed Christmas as her favorite holiday on the *In the Spotlight* bulletin board."

"Maybe she had a bad day," said Dad as he scooped more potatoes onto Jack's plate. "Everyone has a bad day once in a while. Even teachers."

I shook my head. "She's been cranky all week. That's why I'm calling her Miss Crankypants."

"Ah," said Dad. "So when you get cranky, can we call you Miss Crankypants?"

I batted my eyelashes. "I never get cranky. I shine, I sparkle, I . . ."

"Talk too much like Penelope," said Mom.

Crockett glanced at the clock and bit his lip. "He's late. Maybe he's not calling."

Aunt Chrissy patted his arm. "If he said he'd call, he'll call."

Crockett sighed and smashed his peas with his fork.

It drives Mom bonkers when anyone smashes or plays with their food. I tried to kick Crockett under the table to warn him but it was too late.

Mom saw him out of the corner of her eye. She sucked in her breath and started to talk.

This is what I thought she'd say:

"Crockett, no smooshing or smashing your peas. What did they ever do to you? Eat them up. Every last one."

But she didn't say that. This is what she really said:

"I have extra corn bread, Crockett. Would you like another piece?"

Crockett was a lucky duck.

Just then, the phone downstairs rang. Crockett blasted out of his seat. "It's Dad!" He ran down the steps.

A few minutes later, Crockett bounced upstairs and danced around the room. "He'll be here on December twenty-third! You know what else he said?"

"What?" we all asked.

"It's going to be a white Christmas. We're getting snow!"

Snow? I heart snow! I jumped up and danced around with Crockett.

"Maybe we can go into New York and see the tree!" I said. "Then we'll go ice skating at Rockefeller Center." I kicked my leg into the air a few times. "Let's get tickets to see the Rockettes at Radio City Music Hall. It's one of my favorite shows." Then I had the best idea ever. "We'll go to Dylan's Candy Bar and stuff our faces with chocolate-covered caramels."

Crockett stopped dancing. He looked at Aunt Chrissy. Aunt Chrissy looked at me.

"What?" I asked.

Crockett sat. "Well, it's just . . . I haven't seen my dad for a long time. And we sorta want to hang out."

"I know, Crockett," I said. "We'll hang out together."

That's when I saw my mom shake her head from side to side. Then my dad shook his head from side to side. I didn't like head shaking.

"My dad got tickets to the Giants game. We're going into the city to visit the Museum of Natural History and skate in Central Park."

"Guy time," said Aunt Chrissy. "You understand, don't you?"

I understood all right. No Katharine allowed.

For the next ten minutes, Crockett told us everything he was going to

do with his dad over the break while I smoosh, smoosh, smooshed my peas.

Every.

Single.

One.

If we were going to have a white Christmas, then why did I feel so blue?

❀ CHAPTER 3 ❀

Bark, Bark! Meow, Meow!

Mrs. Bingsley was hap, hap, happier the next morning. For snack, she brought in homemade Christmas cookies that everyone could eat. Then we read *The Polar Express* and made jingly bell necklaces.

When Rebecca shrieked, "It's snowing outside!" Mrs. Bingsley didn't get mad like most teachers. Instead, she took us outside so we could catch snowflakes on our tongues.

But in the afternoon, Miss Crankypants returned. She got grumpy when we watched a parent trying to get her car out of the icy parking lot.

"Her wheels can't get traction," said Mrs. Bingsley. "Maybe Mr. Bollwage has some sand he can put under her tires."

Mr. Bollwage is our custodian. He can fix anything! Just then, Mr. Bollwage walked toward the car with a bag over his shoulder.

"There's the sand, Mrs. Bingsley," said Vanessa. "Just like you said."

Mrs. Bingsley smiled. "It's always good to have some sand or gravel in your car. You never know when your wheels will spin in the snow."

"My dad keeps kitty litter in our trunk," said Johnny. "We had to use it last night."

"Meow," said Crockett.

"Meow," said Tamara. Then everyone meowed. Everyone except Mrs. Bingsley.

"That's enough," she said as she pulled the shades down. Then she gave us oodles and oodles of math problems. We did those icky problems for 45 minutes!

Finally, Mrs. Bingsley clapped her hands together. "Music. Line up, please."

We lined up and marched right into music class. I heart music class! Mrs. O'Neil showed us a picture of Wolfie on Santa's lap for the first time.

Wolfie was her son. His real name was Wolfgang Amadeus Mozart O'Neil.

"Is he still howling all the time?" asked Vanessa.

Mrs. O'Neil laughed. "I'm happy to say he's sleeping through the night since you last saw him on Halloween."

She grabbed a bucket of bells and passed them out. "This year, third graders are singing 'Jingle Bells' for our annual holiday sing-along."

Everyone started to shake, shake, shake their bells.

Mrs. O'Neil held up her hand. "Everyone already knows the words to 'Jingle Bells,' but we're going to put a twist on the song."

She pressed a button on her CD player. "Jingle Bells" blasted through the speakers. "Jingle Bells, Jingle Bells, Jingle all the way . . ."

Then something crazy happened. Dogs started to bark and sing "Jingle Bells." "Bark, bark, bark! Bark, bark, bark! Bark, bark, bark, bark, bark!"

Then we heard meows. Vanessa and I laughed. Soon, everyone pretended to be cats as we meowed through the song.

After a minute, Mrs. O'Neil stopped the music. "Won't this be a fun surprise? The other classes will love it." She looked over both shoulders and whispered. "Can we keep it a secret?"

"I'm a super-duper secret keeper," I said.

Vanessa gave me the evil eye.

I ignored her. "Can we tell Mrs. Bingsley?" I asked. "Just Mrs. Bingsley? If I tell her, then I won't even think of blabbing to anyone else."

"Oh, no!" said Mrs. O'Neil. "We're not telling her about it. We're singing it for her when she picks you up."

For the next twenty minutes, we practiced singing our new "Jingle Bells" song. My favorite part was when we barked. I even got a solo! It was only one bark but I'm pretty sure it was the best bark of all!

Mrs. Bingsley picked us up at exactly 2:45. "Ready, class?"

"Not quite," said Mrs. O'Neil. "We have a surprise for you. We're going to give you a preview of our performance."

Mrs. Bingsley clapped her hands. "The sing-along is one of my favorite school activities."

Mrs. O'Neil handed her a bell. "If you get the urge to ring it, feel free."

When our song started, Mrs. Bingsley rang her bell the loudest. She joined in and sang with us. When the barking started, she laughed. She barked with us. I didn't even mind when she sang my solo bark with me. But when we meowed our "Jingle Bells" song, Mrs. Bingsley stopped ringing her bell. Poof! Her smile disappeared.

When we finished, she glanced at her watch. "Let's hurry," she said in a grumpy voice. "The bell's going to ring." She waved to Mrs. O'Neil and marched us right back to our room.

When I walked by her desk, I took a sneak peek to see if there was any glitter left on her desk. Nope! No sprinkles! But I did see something else. On the corner of her desk was an empty picture frame. The frame used to have a picture of her cat, Pumpkin!

My stomach did a flip-flop belly drop. Suddenly I knew why Mrs. Bingsley didn't like my joke or Matthew's story. No wonder she closed the shades after seeing Mr. Bollwage with the kitty litter and stopped singing in music class.

"Crockett," I whispered, "I know why Mrs. Bingsley's been cranky."

A lump rose in my throat.

"You do?" Crockett asked.

I clenched my jaw. "It's a catastrophe!"

❀ CHAPTER 4 ❀

Good Detective Work

"I heard you figured out why Mrs. Bingsley has been so cranky," said Dad during dinner.

"Katharine *thinks* she figured it out," said Crockett.

I glared at Crockett. "It makes sense. Think about the evidence."

Aunt Chrissy rubbed her hands together. "Sounds like a mystery to me. Tell us what happened."

I sucked in my breath. "I think something terrible happened to Pumpkin."

"Pumpkin is her cat," said Crockett.

I took a sip of milk. "The only time Mrs. Bingsley is grumpy is when someone mentions a cat."

"Like what?" asked Mom.

"My joke was about a cat," I said. "Matthew's story was called *The Christmas Cat*. When she saw Mr. Bollwage carrying kitty litter, she got extra grumpy."

"Don't forget music class," said Crockett. "When we barked 'Jingle Bells,' she loved it. But once we had to meow the words, she became Miss Crankypants again."

"Hmmm," said Mom. "That does seem odd."

"But that's not all," I said. "She had a picture of Pumpkin on her desk on Monday. When I looked at the frame today, it was empty. No more Pumpkin!"

"Do you think something happened to the cat?" asked Aunt Chrissy.

I shrugged. "I'm not sure."

"We saw her at the vet last month," said Crockett. "Pumpkin was there for a checkup."

"Maybe Pumpkin ran away," I said. "Can I ask Mrs. Curtin if she knows anything?"

Mrs. Curtin was my kindergarten teacher. She was coming over to tutor me in math.

When the bell rang, I rush-a-rooed into the living room and swung open the door. "Hi, Mrs. Curtin!" I looked down at her feet. Her bunny slippers stared back at me. I gave her a hug.

"It's so nice to see you, Katharine." She took off her coat and hung it on the coatrack. "Your house looks festive! I can see you're ready for Santa."

Mom came to the door. "Hi, there! She sure is ready for Santa. You should see her Christmas list."

"It's this long," I said spreading my arms apart. "I hope Santa brings me a Penelope Parks autographed poster, a Penelope Parks makeup kit, a Penelope Parks music box, a Penelope . . ."

Mrs. Curtin laughed. "I'm sure his elves are busy working on it."

"Katharine set her books up in the dining room. I'm giving Jack a bath so you won't be disturbed," Mom said.

Mrs. Curtin pointed to the macaroni picture frame on the table. "You made that in my class. Look how tiny you look! I remember you and Vanessa tried to eat the macaroni."

Then I remembered Mrs. Bingsley's picture frame! "Can I ask you a question?"

She nodded. "Of course. Is something wrong?"

"There sure is," I said. "But not with me. It's Mrs. Bingsley. It's a catastrophe."

"Oh, my," said Mrs. Curtin with a worried look on her face. "What's wrong? Is she sick?"

I shook my head. Then I told Mrs. Curtin all about Miss Crankypants. But I didn't call her Miss Crankypants. I used my common sense!

"You're right, Katharine. Something did happen to Pumpkin. Mrs. Bingsley

has been down in the dumps about it. She misses him a lot."

I knew it!

"Pumpkin belongs to her sister, Emily. Emily had to move to London for two years. She wasn't allowed to bring Pumpkin. Mrs. Bingsley agreed to watch Pumpkin for Emily. Now that Emily's back, Mrs. Bingsley had to return Pumpkin."

"That's sad," I said. "I feel awful for Miss Crankypants."

"Who?" asked Mrs. Curtin.

Oops. "Did you know that cats have more bones than humans? They have an average of 244 bones. Humans only have 206."

"Really? That is an interesting fact, Katharine. Now how about we work on fractions?"

This is what I wanted to say:

"How can I concentrate on fractions when my super-duper teacher is down in the dumps?"

But this is what I really said:

"What page should I turn to?"

After a lot of eraser dust, tutoring was over! I ran to tell Crockett everything I knew about Pumpkin.

"You were right," said Crockett. "You'd make a good detective."

"We need to do something to make Mrs. Bingsley feel better," I said. "But I don't have any ideas."

Crockett yawned. "Let's talk about it at breakfast. My dad's supposed to call any minute. We're making more plans for Christmas. It's going to be the best Christmas ever!"

I thought about Crockett and his Dad and all the fun they'd have together.

Going to New York.

Without me.

Ice skating in Central Park.

Without me.

Stuffing their faces at Dylan's Candy Bar.

Without me.

Now *I* felt like Miss Crankypants.

CHAPTER 5

Mrs. Ammer to the Rescue!

But Crockett didn't want to talk at breakfast. He was too busy poking his French toast with a fork.

"Crockett and I are coming up with a plan to cheer up Mrs. Bingsley," I announced. "Right, Crockett?"

Crockett didn't say anything. Aunt Chrissy and Mom didn't say anything either.

Crockett poked faster.

Mom raised her eyebrow. "Want a blueberry muffin instead?"

Crockett pushed his plate away. "I'm not hungry."

"Want a waffle with sliced apples?" I asked. I slid the pile toward him. "An apple a day keeps the doctor away."

Crockett threw his napkin down. "I said I'm not hungry. If I didn't want a muffin, I'm not going to eat waffles." He pushed his chair out and grabbed his backpack. "I'll meet you outside."

"What's up with Mr. Crankypants?" I asked. "He needs to turn his frown upside down."

Then I noticed Aunt Chrissy's frowny face.

"Oh, Aunt Chrissy! I was only kidding about calling Crockett Mr. Crankypants."

Aunt Chrissy rubbed my arm. "I know. His father called late last night. It turns out he can't come for Christmas after all."

My eyes lit up. This is what I wanted to say:

"Now Crockett and I can go to New York together and have fun, fun, fun. Who needs Uncle Greg when you can have me, me, me?"

But then I heard Crockett blowing his nose. My stomach did a flip-flop belly drop. So this is what I really said:

"Poor Crockett." I grabbed more tissues and walked outside.

Crockett was leaning against the mailbox kicking the snow.

"I'm sorry, Crockett. Maybe he can come over February break," I said as I slipped him the tissues.

"Maybe." He blew his nose. "Do you mind if we don't talk about it? Let's just tell the kids about Mrs. Bingsley."

So instead of playing four square on the playground before school started, I called all the kids over to the swing set. "We know why Mrs. Bingsley's been so cranky," I said.

"Actually, Katharine figured it out," said Crockett.

I took a bow. No one clapped. "It's about Pumpkin."

"Her cat?" said Vanessa. "What's wrong with Pumpkin?"

"Well," I said. "Pumpkin wasn't really her cat." Then I told them all about Pumpkin and Mrs. Bingsley's sister. "Emily has Pumpkin now."

"So, that's why all the cat things made her so cranky?" asked Rebecca.

"Whew," said Vanessa. "So she wasn't mad at us!"

"Mrs. Curtin said she's down in the dumps," I said. "We need to cheer her up today."

I looked at Crockett. He was down in the dumps, too. I had to figure out a way to cheer him up.

"How do we do that?" asked Matthew.

"By not reading *The Christmas Cat* during Writing Workshop," said Rachel.

"That's right," I said. "No cat stories."

"Or jokes," said Vanessa, looking at Crockett.

"No singing 'Jingle Bells' with meows," said Tamara.

"Why don't we make her a card?" said Diego.

"I'll bring art supplies outside during recess," I said. "Maybe I can sneak my markers outside."

When the bell rang, we were ready to help Mrs. Bingsley forget all about her cat troubles.

It worked!

Matthew read *Santa's Trip to the Moon* during Writing Workshop. Mrs. Bingsley said she would love to visit the moon with Santa.

When we had to make a chart and graph our favorite animals during math, no one picked a C-A-T. Crockett wasn't in the mood to tell jokes. But Tamara sure was. She told three Christmas jokes. Mrs. Bingsley said they were clever . . . just like her!

But on the way to recess, I saw something terrible on the wall by the office. Something that would make Mrs. Bingsley sad. Since I was the last in line, I stayed behind looking at it all by myself.

Come see the musical Cats *at Villagers Community Theater!*

Tickets are $5.00 each. Bring the whole family.

January 10-18. See you there!

I groaned. Mrs. Bingsley would not be happy if she saw this! I looked to the left. I looked to the right. I knew what I had to do. A minute later, I was sitting comfy cozy in the principal's office.

I leaned forward and said, "I need your help, Mrs. Ammer."

Mrs. Ammer pulled her seat closer to me. "You look so serious, Katharine. How can I help you?"

"You need to take that *Cats* poster off of the wall ASSSP."

"You mean ASAP? As soon as possible?" said Mrs. Ammer. She sighed. "I'm just tickled pink you didn't rip it down yourself!"

Silly Mrs. Ammer. Didn't she know that I didn't deface school property anymore?

"We have a catastrophe on our hands!" I said. Then I told her all about Mrs. Bingsley and Pumpkin.

"I remember the day Emily adopted Pumpkin. I was volunteering at Happy Tails back then," Mrs. Ammer told me.

"The animal shelter?" I asked. "That's where Vanessa got her dog, Sparky!"

Mrs. Ammer nodded. "Lots of people adopt animals from Happy Tails. It's a wonderful organization." Then she smiled. "So you and your friends are making Mrs. Bingsley a card? That will cheer her up. It's a great plan. And about the poster . . ."

But I wasn't listening. I had a new plan. A better-than-making-a-card-for-Mrs.-Bingsley plan.

I told Mrs. Ammer all about it.

"What a wonderful, thoughtful idea, Katharine. I'm so proud of you."

"Don't tell Mrs. Bingsley. Promise?"

She walked over and gave me a great big hug. "Promise. Your secret is safe with me. I'll check with your mom and see if it's okay. If it is, I'll call Vanessa's mother and your Aunt Chrissy, too. If they all agree to it, I'll meet the three of you back here at dismissal."

"Great!" I said. As I left her office, I giggled. "Don't let the cat out of the bag!"

❀ CHAPTER 6 ❀

Happy Tails

"Where were you?" asked Crockett.

"We were waiting to make Mrs. Bingsley a card," said Vanessa.

"Sorry." I shoved the markers back in my desk. "Can both of you keep a secret?"

Vanessa clapped. "You know I can."

Crockett sighed. His eyes were red. Finally, he nodded.

"I have a per-fect-o idea! I know what we can do to cheer up Mrs. Bingsley. Mrs. Ammer is going to help us."

"Mrs. Ammer?" said Crockett. He cracked a smile for the first time. "How did she get involved?"

"I'll tell you later," I told them. "But she's taking us someplace special after school. She's calling both of your moms now. If they say you can go, will you?"

"I have nothing else to do," said Crockett. He shoved his hands in his pockets. "Nothing at all."

"I love surprises!" said Vanessa. "I won't tell anyone. Promise!"

At 3:45, we pulled into the parking lot of Happy Tails.

"We're here!" I shouted.

Crockett's eyes lit up. "Are you adopting a pet, Mrs. Ammer?"

I looked at Crockett. "No, silly goose. We are!"

Vanessa's mouth flew open. "I just got Sparky. My mom won't let me adopt another pet."

"We're adopting a pet for Mrs. Bingsley," I said. "Hello, kitty cat! Goodbye, Miss Crankypants!"

Mrs. Ammer raised her eyebrows. "I'll pretend I didn't hear that!"

Two minutes later, we were inside looking at the rows of cages.

Crockett stopped in front of the third cage. "It's a Siamese cat. It's so cute!"

Miss Lucy, the owner, opened the cage but the cat wouldn't budge. "She's shy."

She told us to sit on the floor while she opened more cages. A minute later, the room was full of cats.

"Are all of these cats waiting to get adopted?" asked Mrs. Ammer.

Miss Lucy sighed. "Yep. We're trying to find a good home for all of them."

A kitten played with my shoelace. "We know someone who would make a great cat owner."

Vanessa and Crockett agreed.

"Are they free?" asked Crockett as he scooped up a black cat. "Can anyone adopt one?"

"Sparky was free. Sort of," said Vanessa as she stroked two cats who were sleeping in her lap. "We gave a donation to the shelter last month."

"I thought I recognized you!" said Miss Lucy. "Vanessa's right. We ask for donations to help with the cost of taking care of the

animals. We need to be able to provide food for them." She pointed to the door. "Our dogs are in that room."

Crockett got up and peeked through the glass window.

"We go through a lot of kitty litter, dog bones, paper towels, and food each month. We also try to buy a few toys to keep the animals happy."

Miss Lucy turned toward Mrs. Ammer. "The donations have slowed down a lot. I've been buying the food lately."

"Oh, Lucy!" said Mrs. Ammer. "I'm sorry to hear that. You've spent so much of your own money on the animals."

"They're like family," said Miss Lucy. "That's why I work so hard to find them good homes. Are you interested in another cat?"

"It's not for her," I said. "It's for our teacher, Mrs. Bingsley. We want to surprise her with a kitten. Mrs. Ammer said she'd help us."

"We ask for a fifty dollar donation for kittens. But if you don't have it, that's okay. As long as I know Mrs. Bingsley will provide a good home."

"But we do have the money," said Crockett. "Well, we'll have money soon."

Vanessa and I stared at each other.

"We do?" said Vanessa. "We will?"

"We can get it," said Crockett. "When Mrs. Bingsley said we couldn't have a Secret Santa, we were upset. Maybe it was a good thing. We can use our Secret Santa money for the donation."

I patted Crockett on the back. "What a super-duper idea!"

"It's about $100," said Crockett.

"You'll have money left over," said Miss Lucy.

Vanessa shook her head. "We don't need the money. You should keep it and buy cat food. Maybe some cat toys for Christmas."

Miss Lucy's eyes got watery. "What a caring bunch of kids, Mrs. Ammer. You should be proud of them. That extra fifty dollars will mean a lot to all of the animals at Happy Tails. That will be enough money to buy a week's worth of cat food."

"Only a week?" I asked. "That's not a very long time. What will you do then?"

"We'll manage," said Miss Lucy. "We always do."

That's when I got another idea. A we'll-show-Miss-Lucy-just-how-caring-we-really-are idea.

Naughty or Nice?

"It certainly seems like you had an exciting afternoon," said Dad. "I'm proud of you, Katharine. You too, Crockett."

Crockett smiled. Sort of.

"We picked out the cutest kitten for Mrs. Bingsley," I said. "Mrs. Ammer is taking care of it until we give it to her at the sing-along. It was Crockett's idea to collect five dollars from everyone."

"That's my Crockett," said Aunt Chrissy. "Always thinking."

Mom put a clean bib on Jack. "It's nice to think of others during the holidays, isn't it? Giving a gift always feels better than getting a gift."

"I'm sure this puts both of you on the top of Santa's Nice List," said Aunt Chrissy.

Crockett rolled his eyes. "I know who's on top of the Naughty List."

"Is it Johnny?" I asked. "He did put a spider on Rebecca's desk."

"Nope," said Crockett.

I scratched my head. "Is it Diego? He chews gum in class every day."

"It's not him," said Crockett.

I thought about my three missed homework assignments and the glitter sprinkles on Mrs. Bingsley's desk. My palms started to sweat. Did Crockett know I borrowed his math homework last week?

"Is it me?" I asked. I crossed my fingers. I just had to be on Santa's Nice List.

"It's not you, Katharine," said Crockett. "Don't worry."

"Well, then who is it?" I asked. "I just gotta know."

"Yeah," said Aunt Chrissy. "Don't leave us hanging."

Crockett got up and wiped his eyes. "Dad."

Before Aunt Chrissy could stop him, he ran downstairs.

"Why can't Uncle Greg come?" I asked. "Doesn't he want to see Crockett?"

"Of course he does," said Aunt Chrissy. "He feels terrible about it."

Now Aunt Chrissy played with her food! "He has two conference calls that he can't miss. One is on Christmas Eve and the other is a few days after Christmas."

"Can't he call them from here?" I asked.

Aunt Chrissy sighed. "That was what I thought. But he has a special computer he needs to use. He can't travel with it."

I swung my feet back and forth under the table. The harder I thought, the faster they went. "Hey! I have an idea. Can Crockett go to his house instead?"

"Plane tickets to California are so expensive, especially during the holidays. I can't afford a ticket and neither can Crockett's father. His ticket was non-refundable," Aunt Chrissy explained.

"Chrissy," said Dad, "our offer still stands."

"Let us help," said Mom.

Aunt Chrissy hugged Mom and Dad. "You've already done so much for us since the divorce. I simply can't take anything else from either one of you."

But she can take it from me, I thought.

When Aunt Chrissy went to check on Crockett, I told my parents my plan.

"You want to *what*?" asked Dad. "That's a big chunk of change."

"I want to buy Crockett his plane ticket," I repeated. "I have money from Pop Pop."

"No one expects you to use your money, Katharine," said Mom. "Besides, you could buy a lot of Penelope Parks lip gloss with that money." She started to clear the dishes. Dad stretched and yawned.

"I'm serious," I said. But they weren't listening to me!

What would Penelope do? I stood at the table and tap, tap, tapped my spoon against a glass. They ignored me. I stood up on a kitchen chair and cleared my throat. "I insist on buying Crockett's ticket, Mother."

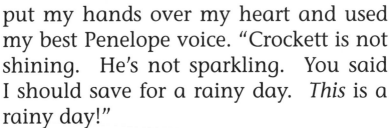

They both turned around and stared at me. "Yes, Father, you heard me. I insist on doing this good deed for my dear cousin, Crockett."

Now I wanted to act even more dramatic. I put my hands over my heart and used my best Penelope voice. "Crockett is not shining. He's not sparkling. You said I should save for a rainy day. *This* is a rainy day!"

"Okay, Penelope," said Dad. "Have you really thought about this?"

"It's too much money," said Mom. But Dad stopped her.

"Haven't we always said we wanted Katharine to make the world a little bit brighter?"

Mom looked confused. But she admitted, "I suppose so."

I jumped off the chair. "Crockett's not only my cousin. He's my best friend, Mom. If I didn't get to see one of you for Christmas, I'd cry for days. I really, really, really, really want to do this."

Five minutes later, we printed the ticket from the computer.

I jumped three times in front of the kitchen sink. That's my signal to Crockett that I need him speedy quick.

Aunt Chrissy came up instead. "Crockett doesn't feel like coming up. Sorry."

"Then we'll just have to go down and see him," said Mom. She grabbed my hand and dragged me down the steps.

"Is it safe?" I asked. "Are the critters out of sight?" I opened my eyes. Right in front of me were two tanks. Tanks full of critters. Creepy, crawly critters. As much as I love Crockett, I do not like his critters. Not one bit.

"What are you doing down here?" asked Crockett. He blew his nose.

I flung my arms around him. "Merry Christmas, Crockett. This is my gift to you." I pushed the paper under his nose.

It took him a minute to realize what it was. "A plane ticket?"

"You got that right!" I said as I jumped up and down and clapped my hands. "Now you can have the best Christmas ever."

"Katharine bought you the ticket with her own money," said Mom. "It was her idea."

I wrinkled my nose. "What would I do with the money anyway?"

Crockett raised his eyebrows. "Buy fifty bottles of Penelope Parks nail polish and thirty tubes of lip gloss."

"Lip gloss, schlip gloss," I said. "Who needs it?"

"Thanks, Katharine," said Crockett as he hugged me. "I'm the happiest kid in the world today!"

"And tomorrow," I said, "Mrs. Bingsley will be the happiest teacher once she gets her new kitten."

A hissing sound came from one of the tanks. "I gotta get out of here."

"Why?" asked Crockett.

I ran up the stairs and shouted, "Because I'm a scaredy cat!"

❀ CHAPTER 8 ❀

Jingle Bells

Everyone wore dressy clothes for the sing-along. Mrs. Ammer bought each kid a Santa hat to wear. Even Mrs. Curtin's bunny slippers had two teeny tiny Santa hats on top!

"Are you going up on the stage with us to sing 'Jingle Bells'?" asked Crockett.

Mrs. Bingsley pulled up a chair beside him. "I think I'll sit this one out. 'Jingle Bells' isn't one of my favorite songs." She twisted her ring a few times and sunk down in the chair.

I jumped up and hugged Mrs. Bingsley. "I think you're going to want to sing with us today. Be ready!"

"Maybe I'll sing the traditional 'Jingle Bells' song. Honestly, I don't care for all that barking and meowing."

Vanessa giggled. She gave Crockett and me two thumbs-up.

Mrs. O'Neil stepped up to the microphone. "Let's start off our sing-along with 'We Wish You A Merry Christmas.'"

The whole school joined in, including Mrs. Bingsley.

Then Mrs. O'Neil introduced the kindergartners. They sang "Up on the Housetop," "The Dreidel Song," and "Rudolph the Red-Nosed Reindeer."

Finally, it was our turn to go up on stage. When we stepped onto the risers, Mrs. Ammer took the microphone from Mrs. O'Neil.

"Before the third graders sing, I want to take a moment to thank each and every one of them for being so caring, giving, and generous."

Mrs. Bingsley shifted in her seat. She looked confused.

"Mrs. Bingsley, would you mind joining your students up here for a minute?"

Mrs. Bingsley walked slowly up the stairs.

Mrs. Ammer put her arm around Mrs. Bingsley. "Your students are truly remarkable. I think they've had a wonderful role model. Don't you agree, kids?"

Everyone clapped and cheered.

"They've noticed that you seemed a little down in the dumps lately. They wanted to do something to cheer you up." She scanned the risers until she saw me.

"Katharine, would you please join us?" Mrs. Ammer said.

I hopped down the risers and raced over to Mrs. Ammer. I took a quicky quick bow when I reached the microphone.

Everyone laughed.

Even Mrs. Bingsley.

I took the microphone. "Mrs. Bingsley, we all chipped in our Secret Santa money to get you an extra special Christmas gift. We hope you like it. We know it will like you!"

Crockett and Vanessa came out from behind the curtain. They carried a big green box topped with a red bow.

"This is for you," said Crockett.

"It's from all of us," said Vanessa. "We know you're going to love it."

Mrs. Bingsley's hands shook. "I don't know what to say. What should I do?"

"Open it!" screamed the audience.

Mrs. Bingsley gasped when she lifted the lid off the box. "A kitten! A lovely little kitten!" She held it up for all to see. She started to cry. "How did you know?"

"We're Santa's little helpers," I said.

At that moment, Mrs. O'Neil started to play "Jingle Bells" on the piano. Everyone started to sing. When we got to the barking part, the kids barked with us. When we started to meow, everyone else did, too. Even Mrs. Bingsley.

When the music stopped, everyone clapped. Someone shouted, "Encore! Encore!"

It was Mrs. Bingsley!

We sang the songs again. When we finished, Mrs. Bingsley dabbed her eyes with a tissue. "You've made this such a special Christmas. I'm the happiest person in the world right now!"

I high-fived Crockett. "Told you!"

"Jingle Bells and I will be very happy together!" said Mrs. Bingsley. "Very, very happy!"

Everyone started to sing "Jingle Bells" again.

Before the fourth graders came up, Mrs. Ammer explained all about adopting pets from Happy Tails.

"It's a good place that needs our help," Mrs. Ammer said. "That's why our January community service project will be to collect dog and cat food, paper towels, kitty litter, and small toys for the shelter."

Someone yelled out, "Great idea, Mrs. Ammer!"

Mrs. Ammer held up her hand for everyone to be quiet. "It is a good idea, isn't it? I wish I could say it was my idea but it wasn't. It was Katharine Marie

Carmichael's idea. Let's give her a round of applause."

Mrs. Bingsley held Jingle Bells close to her heart. Then she leaned over and whispered something that made me feel sparkly and shiny.

"Katharine Marie Carmichael, you're the cat's meow!"

Crockett's Holiday HaHaHas

Do you know someone who's acting like Miss Crankypants? Make them laugh with one of these jokes!

Q. Where does a snowman keep his money?
A. In a snow bank.

Q. What do you get when you cross a snowman and a vampire?
A. Frostbite.

Q. Why is Santa so good at karate?
A. Because he has a black belt.

Q. What did the monkey sing on Christmas day?
A. "Jungle bells, Jungle bells. . ."

Q. What did Jack Frost say to Frosty the Snowman?
A. "Have an ice day!"